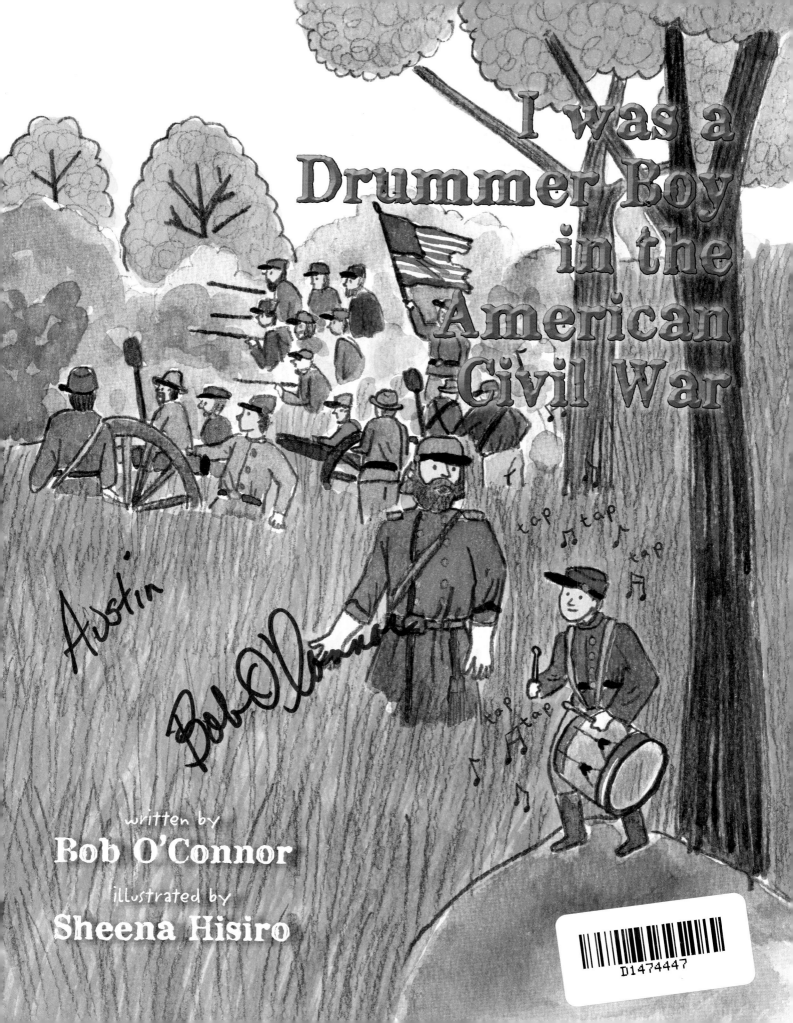

I was a Drummer Boy in the American Civil War

written by
Bob O'Connor

illustrated by
Sheena Hisiro

This book is dedicated to my maternal Great-Uncle Michael Minnihan who fought bravely in Captain Terry's Company E of the 105th Illinois Infantry.
- Bob O'Connor

To mom and dad
- Sheena Hisiro

Bob O'Connor Books LLC © Copyright 2018
Illustrations copyright © 2018 by Sheena Hisiro
Graphic Design by Sheena Hisiro

This is historical fiction though every character is real and the situations all happened to the 105th Illinois Infantry.

Foreword

The most important job for a Civil War drummer boy was to pound out the officer's commands on his drum loud enough that the troop could hear the orders above the loud noises of the battles.

Both Union and Confederate troops attacked, retreated, or moved into position when they heard a certain beat from the drummer.

The drummer had to learn and practice each beat. His place in battle was to stand right next to the officer in charge. The officer told the command to the drummer. The drummer beat out the message to the troops.

Yes, the drummer boy was quite young, but he had a very large job. He was also in the direct line of fire from the enemy.

This story is about the drummer of the 105th Illinois Infantry, USA. But it could have been the story of most every other drummer during the American Civil War.

August 1862
Dixon, Illinois

My name *is* James R. Minnihan. I am eleven years old.

My uncle, Michael Minnihan, who lived in nearby Alto, Illinois had presented me with my own drum, drumsticks, and Mr. Howe's "United States Regulation Drum and Fife Instructor" book for my birthday last September. I have been practicing my drumming ever since. I now know every single drum beat that went with every military order. Since I was good at drumming, I felt my uncle's regiment could use me.

September 1, 1862

My Uncle Michael marched to my hometown of Dixon for training with the 105th Illinois Infantry. I asked my mother and father if I could join them. I wanted to help save the country too.

They told me I was too young to go. I fought back tears. I was too young to go but too old to cry. I bit my lip instead. I was sad. I thought I needed to do my part.

September 8, 1862

     Last night I dreamed of joining as the regimental drummer boy. I had learned from my uncle that the drummer's job was to use the rat-a-tat-tat of his drum to pass the orders from the officer to the troops. Often the officers' orders could not be heard above the noise of the battles. The drummer boy had an important job in each army.

     I woke from my dream before the sun had come up. I had made my decision. I quietly gathered my drum and drumsticks, Mr. Howe's book, and snuck downstairs. I wrote a note to my parents.

Dear mother and father,
   I have decided to join the 105th Illinois Infantry as a drummer. I know you will be disappointed that I have left against your wishes, but Mr. Lincoln needs me too.
   I hope I will make you proud. I intend to be the best drummer ever. You will be missed greatly. I love you.

   Your son,
   James

That same morning

I carried my drum, my drumsticks, my book, and placed the few dollars I had saved up in my pocket. I wasn't on the streets for more than a minute when I determined perhaps I should have planned this out. I knew I needed to find the 105th Illinois Infantry, but had no idea where they were. I walked to the bridge and crossed the Rock River into the downtown area.

My neighbor, Mr. Henry, came by in a wagon. He called to me. "Where are you headed so early in the morning, lad?"

"To join my Uncle Michael and the 105th Illinois Infantry," I said loudly, trying to act brave and sound like I knew what I was doing.

"Good for you, Jimmy," Mr. Henry said. "The country needs fine boys like you. Do you know where the soldiers are?" he asked.

"No sir" I replied, trying to not cry and give myself away.

"They are leaving this morning for Camp Douglas in Chicago. I guess you need to get to the train station quickly before they leave without you. Here. Jump in. Ole Bess and I will give you a ride."

I climbed on board, handing my drum up to him first. And I thanked him for his help.

"By helping you, I'm doing my part for my country," he explained. And then he asked "Do you have money for the train ticket?"

"Yes, sir. I do."

In no time, Mr. Henry delivered me to the Dixon train station. I was in luck. The train had not left.

Mr. Henry saluted me like I was a real soldier. I returned his salute. He wished me "God Speed". I thanked him again. And I wondered if he was going to go to my house next to tell my mother and father where I was going.

I found Uncle Michael at the train station. He was surprised to see me. I was afraid he would send me home.

"Are you ready to go to war with us, James?" he asked.

"Yes, sir," I said loudly.

"I will help get you that drummer's job you want so badly," he promised.

September 16, 1862

At Camp Douglas, we got blue uniforms and started drilling. My uniform was a tad too big for me. But I wore it proudly anyway.

I knew Uncle Michael would ask the big question. And he asked it today.

"James. Does your mother know you are here?"

"Yes, sir," I told him bravely and then added, "I left her a note."

Uncle Michael didn't look very happy about that. "Hmmmmm. I'm thinking I need to send her a note telling her that I promise to keep an eye on you. Is that alright with you, soldier?"

"Yes, sir. Thank you, Uncle Michael."

October 2, 1862

We traveled in cattle cars on the train from Chicago, Illinois to Louisville, Kentucky, arriving this day. Our training was to continue here.

I drummed my way around camp each day during the marching and drilling. I drummed loudly every single order I had learned so that whoever was listening would know that I could be counted on when the time came.

Captain Terry, the commanding officer of Company E, found me. He welcomed me to his company. He told me how impressed everyone in camp had been with my expert drumming. He asked if I knew the seriousness of my job in his company. I told him "Yes, sir."

He said when we moved into a battle, I needed to be just a few feet away from him at all times. When things got bad, he didn't want to have to go looking for me.

"I promise, sir, to be with you at all times. I will be ready." With that he saluted me and left.

Winter 1862 - 1863

Every single day I woke up ready for action. Most days there was none. I was treated no differently than any other soldier except in extreme circumstances, like when they needed to carry me across the river at the ford because the water was over my head. Most other times, I was on equal footing with everyone else.

No one treated me as if I were too young to be here. They knew their company needed their drummer to be reliable when the time came. I made sure they knew that they had no worries about my job. They just needed to worry about their jobs.

Uncle Michael checked up on me almost every day. Several times he brought along letters to me from my mother. As you might have guessed, she was still not happy that I was a soldier. She told me at my age I should have been having fun, not fighting wars.

I did not tell her I was having great fun here. I also felt I was doing something very important.

1863

The entire year found us marching to and fro, from Nashville, Tennessee to Murphreesboro, back to Nashville, to Stevenson, Alabama to Shelbyville, Tennessee, and every place in between.

I trained and drilled, marched and rested, and trained some more. Sadly, I attended funerals of sick soldiers who died along the way.

I helped put up and tear down pontoon bridges and build plank roads. I learned how to play cards and survive days on end with just coffee and hardtack.

We were trained to be a fighting army but had not found any battles even after a whole year of marching. But we were always ready for action, no matter what we were doing.

May 15, 1864

When it came time for my first battle, I was ready. That day was today. I kept in 1st Lt. Allen's shadow (he was our new commanding officer). He reminded me that in the noise of the battle, it would be my loud drumming not his shouts that would carry his orders to the troops in the field. With the very loud noises from the cannons never stopping for an instant, I pounded loudly with the rat-a-tat tat of my drum letting the soldiers know what their commanding officer ordered them to do.

With the bullets and cannon balls flying, you might think I was afraid. But I wasn't. I was too busy trying to do my job to be worried.

At the end of the day, I was tired beyond any tired I had ever felt. But the noise had ended and the battle had been won. 1st Lt. Allen saluted me and said, "James, you were great out there today. Not one of my company carried on any better than you did. Thank you."

Uncle Michael found me back in camp. "The men were grateful for your excellent service today. They wanted me to tell you. With all the loud noises today, we never would have heard the orders. We are grateful to you, soldier." He saluted me.

I was happy that I had made my uncle proud of my work.

I tended to my duties through small battles and large battles and days of no battles at all. I admit I was homesick, but I never wanted to go home. I was doing my part to save the country -- even if it was a little part done by a little soldier. My only complaint was the noise of the battles was almost too much for me.

During the action, I never looked up. I had no idea if we were winning or losing. I had to concentrate on the job I had to do. Other soldiers asked if I wasn't afraid of getting killed in the battles. I had never given it a thought. They asked if I was scared. I was not scared. I was proud.

We trained on the days when there were no battles. Those days were much more often than days when we fought. Our officers wanted us to be ready for most anything. Soldiers talked about being tired and homesick. I was just as tired and probably just as homesick. But I felt like I was doing my part for Mr. Lincoln.

At night, I dreamed of meeting Mr. Lincoln someday and showing him my fine drum.

July 4th, 1864
Regimental Band Concert
Marietta, Georgia

I was really proud tonight. I was invited to sit in with the 105th Illinois Regimental Band as they played patriotic tunes to help celebrate Independence Day, the 4th of July.

We played songs like "Yankee Doodle Dandy", "When Johnny Comes Marching Home Again", "John Brown's Body", and others.

Late summer 1864
Georgia

Our biggest enemy this summer has been rain. We saw much more rain than enemy soldiers. It has rained and rained, and then rained some more. It was not easy to march in the rain and mud.

I worried more for my drum than for myself. I had to make sure each evening that my drum was clean and dry.

I am not much use to the army if my drum was not in good working condition.

September 2, 1864

Today we marched into Atlanta as part of General Sherman's army. There were no soldiers there to fight us. It was said that the size of our army had scared off those rebel boys.

We rested for a few days. We were told that our next stop would be Savannah, Georgia.

I got a chance to rest a bit. Today I wrote another letter to my mother and father so they would not worry about me.

December 21, 1864
The Surrender of Savannah

There was no rebel army to keep us from capturing Savannah either. After many battles and important jobs to do, I was not needed much here. But I proudly pounded on my drum leading our company into this southern city.

November 9, 1864

We didn't stay in Savannah very long. We began to march north today.

We marched with General Slocum who was leader of the Twentieth Corps (which the 105th Illinois was part of) and the Fifteenth Corps.

We hadn't seen hide nor hare of the enemy in recent days. But we always remained ready.

At night, I slept well because the marching made me very tired.

April 11, 1865

We learned today that Confederate General Robert E. Lee had surrendered two days go. There was celebration in our camp. We were also reminded that our job was not finished, because the enemy in our area had not surrendered. We were ordered to be alert.

April 16, 1865

We were told today that President Lincoln had been killed. Our celebration from the news of the surrender turned to sadness with this news.

April 26, 1865

Confederate General Johnston surrendered to General Sherman today at Bennett Place, North Carolina. This signaled the end of the long war. We would soon be going home.

The regimental band played. There was much celebration in camp.

Our next march would be to Washington City before being sent home.

May 24, 1865

    After arriving in Washington City on
May 19, we prepared to look our best. I washed
my uniform, polished my buttons, and scrubbed
my drum.

    Today we marched with the Twentieth
Corps in the victory parade of the Grand Army
of the Potomac.

June 17, 1865

    We arrived back at the train station in Dixon, Illinois today. My mother and father were waiting for me to welcome me home.

    I was happy to see them and happy to be back home.

    I was proud that I had served to help save the Union.

Historic Note

James R. Minnehan (his name was later changed to Minnihan) was born September 9, 1851 in Oswego, Illinois. His uncle, Michael Minnihan, was the older brother of my maternal great-grandfather, Dominick Minnihan.

Acknowledgements

Thanks to Trish Lombard, a direct descendent of Michael Minnihan, for her contributions to this project.

Thanks to Carl Hisiro for suggesting if I ever needed an illustrator for an upcoming project, I might consider his daughter. Great idea Carl!! Thanks also for noticing some corrections needed in the manuscript.

Thanks to my sister, Joanne White, my daughter, Kelli, and my family for their love, support, and encouragement each and every day of my career as a writer.

Thanks to wonderful teacher, Rebecca Boreczky, for her gentle nudges that led to my career in publishing.

And special kudos to my great new illustrator, Sheena Hisiro, for her fabulous drawings in this book. Terrific job!!!!!

Author

Bob O'Connor has been writing since early elementary school. His first published article was in 1959 in the Illinois Junior Historical Magazine. He has now published fourteen books, mostly about the American Civil War. This is his first, but not last, children's book.

For more info, visit:
www.boboconnorbooks.com

Illustrator

Sheena Hisiro has been drawing since she could hold a pencil. She has a BFA in Communications Design from Pratt Institute. She has illustrated more than 35 books including *The Boy Who Cried Wolf!*, *I'm Rascal*, and *Matushka Z.'s Very Russian Looking Hat*.

For more info, visit:
oodlesofdoodles.tumblr.com

COMING SOON

My second children's book, the story of a blind boy who helped save the Union. The star of the book will be my grandson, Kyle, who is a student of Maryland School for the Blind in Belair, Maryland.

Bob O'Connor
Bob O'Connor Books
www.boboconnorbooks.com
author@boboconnorbooks.com

- Host of "The Chronicles of the American Civil War" podcast
- Named finalist four times in National Book competition
- Award winner in WV Press Association competition
- Speaker, historian, researcher, and author